Shaggy Dog's Tall Tale

written and illustrated by
Donald Charles

CHILDRENS PRESS, CHICAGO

for yvonne

Library of Congress Cataloging in Publication Data

Charles, Donald.
  Shaggy Dog's tall tale.

  SUMMARY: Shaggy Dog tells Calico Cat what happened
to him when he fell into a deep puddle on a rainy day.
  [1. Animals—Fiction] I. Title.
PZ7.C374Sh   [E]   79-26493
ISBN 0-516-03616-5

6 7 8 9 10 11 R 93 92 91 90 89

Shaggy Dog's
Tall Tale

4

"Here's my tall tale," Shaggy Dog said to Calico Cat.

"One rainy day
I fell into a
deep puddle!

At the bottom of the
puddle I found
a bank of
sand dollars.

9

I took a nap in an
oyster bed. A crab
woke me up.

I chased a catfish.

I fell over a
waterfall and
saw starfish.

A turtle gave
me a ride.

I danced at a fish ball.

19

An electric eel
bit my toe.

I floated out of
the puddle in a
whale bubble.

An elephant took
me in his trunk.

The elephant sneezed,
and I found myself
home in bed."

Shaggy Dog said
"That's my tall tale."

29

"I don't believe more
than half of it,"
sniffed Calico Cat.

31

Shaggy Dog can make up stories. Can you?

ABOUT THE AUTHOR/ARTIST

Donald Charles started his long career as an artist and author more than twenty-five years ago after attending the University of California and the Art League School of California. He began by writing and illustrating feature articles for the San Francisco Chronicle, and also sold cartoons and ideas to The New Yorker and Cosmopolitan magazines. Since then he has been, at various times, a longshoreman, ranch hand, truck driver, and editor of a weekly newspaper, all enriching experiences for a writer and artist. Ultimately he became creative director for an advertising agency, a post which he resigned several years ago to devote himself full-time to book illustration and writing. Mr. Charles has received frequent awards from graphic societies, and his work has appeared in numerous textbooks and periodicals.